What Goes Around · Comes Around ·

What Goes Around

EMPIRE MARKET

DOUBLEDAY

NEW YORK   LONDON   TORONTO   SYDNEY   AUCKLAND

...Comes Around

By SALLY G. WARD

PUBLISHED BY DOUBLEDAY
a division of Bantam Doubleday Dell Publishing Group, Inc.
666 Fifth Avenue, New York, New York 10103

LIBRARY OF CONGRESS CATALOGING-IN-PUBLICATION DATA
Ward, Sally G.
What goes around comes around / Sally G. Ward.—1st ed.
   p.   cm.
Summary: Isabel accompanies her unusual grandmother on a fun-
filled journey through the neighborhood to give away soup.
[1. Grandmothers—Fiction.   2. Neighborliness—Fiction.]
I. Title.
PZ7.W2158Wh   1991
[E]—dc20   89-71393   CIP   AC

DOUBLEDAY
and the portrayal of an anchor with a dolphin are trademarks of Doubleday,
a division of Bantam Doubleday Dell Publishing Group, Inc.

ISBN 0-385-41222-3
ISBN 0-385-41223-1 (lib. bdg.)
Copyright © 1991 by Sally G. Ward
RL: 2.3

Designed by Barbara DuPree Knowles

This is me, Isabel,
with my mama.
In our own little apartment,
in the North End.

And this is my
Grandma Rose,
in her apartment
not too far away
from Mama and me.

Grandma Rose wears high-top sneakers,
and keeps an ornery old parrot named Fred, who swears.
Grandma says he reminds her of an old boyfriend.

For her work, my Grandma Rose sews for other people.
They come from all over the city to have my Grandma Rose
make things for them. That's what she does for work.

For fun, she makes soups. The soup cooks while she sews,
and while she tap-dances, and while she sees to Fred.
Sometimes her soup is still cooking even when she is resting.

When the soup is finally done,
Grandma Rose spoons it out into
jars of all shapes and sizes,
and packs them up in her old green bag.

Then she puts a CLOSED sign
on the door, and takes
the soup around to people.
Sometimes they're her friends;
sometimes they're strangers.
That's what she does for fun.

"Your Grandma Rose is different," said my mama.
"If she's got it, she has to give some away."

"Was she always like that?" I asked.

"Long as I can remember," Mama told me.

"So how did you live? There's hardly any furniture at Grandma Rose's."

"That was the first to go," Mama said. " 'What do we need with things?'
your Grandma Rose would ask us. Maybe one day you can go along
with her when she takes her soups around."

The very next week Mama got sick.

"She has the flu," said the doctor, "and she's not to get out of bed for the whole day. No going to work, no nothing."

We called Grandma.

"I'll shut off my machine,
give Fred some water,
put up the CLOSED sign,
and be right over,"
said Grandma Rose.
"And today, my Isabel,
you come with me."

When Grandma came over,
she went straight to Mama's bed.

"Oh, my poor baby. I brought over some soup. Are you warm enough?
You feel hot. What did the doctor say? So what does he know.
You rest, my cupcake. Drink lots of fluids. Isabel, get your mama
some fresh water," said Grandma, all in one breath.

Grandma and I went to
my room to get my coat.
"Isabel," she said, "you're
an artist. Such a talent
you've got, I can't believe.
You remind me of your mama
when she was little.
Pictures. Always pictures.
Everywhere pictures. Did you
ever think of giving some away?"

I gave Mama my blanket, for company, and Grandma
gave her a bowl of soup, for strength.

Then I got my pennies in case I saw
something special for Mama.
Or maybe something special for Grandma Rose.

"Ta-ta, my sweet one," said my Grandma Rose.

"Bye-bye, Mama," said I.

"Where are we going, Grandma?" I asked right away.

"First to Mr. Cataloni," answered Grandma Rose. "His wife Sophia has been gone so long he is lonely. Maybe my soup will cheer him up. Besides, I have to pick out some vegetables for my soup, and the best place for *fresh* is Mr. Cataloni's."

Mr. Cataloni runs the Empire Market on Charles Street. I love to go there, because Mr. Cataloni has hair that grows out of his ears. Grandma Rose tells me not to stare.

Grandma Rose greeted
Mr. Cataloni as if she
hadn't seen him for years.

"Isabel is helping me today," Grandma
explained. "I am so lucky. Her poor
mama is not so lucky, I think.
She is home sick. The flu."

"Isabel. *Bella* Isabella. Pick out something special for you
poor sick mama. I give you. Pick out two somethings.
I give you two. Because you Grandma Rose make me such soup.
Deliziosa," said Mr. Cataloni.

"Carmine, did I mention my soup?" asked Grandma Rose.

"No, Mrs. D. With my ears, I hear nothing. But with my eyes,
I see the bag," said Mr. Cataloni, his eyes twinkling.

"Ah, a detective he is now,"
said Grandma Rose, laughing.

Mr. Cataloni laughed too.
"I am a very happy detective,"
he said, "because my Sophia
is finally coming home
from her mama's."

"Wonderful, Carmine," said my grandma. "So maybe you don't want any of my soup this time?"

"Rose, *bellissima donna*," said Mr. Cataloni. "The day I don't want any of your soup is the day I stop breathing." Then he kissed my Grandma Rose's glove.

I picked out the shiniest red apple and the ripest orange for my mama, just as Mr. Cataloni told me.

Grandma Rose was inside paying for her vegetables when Mr. Cataloni handed me a fat, wrapped-up package.

"For you and you grandma who loves you, Isabella. Some hard rolls and cheese. You and Grandma take this to the park and have a nice bit of lunch with these, no? And you think of Mr. Cataloni, and how happy he is having sips of you Grandma Rosa's soups. And when you done, maybe you give the birdies a nice bit of crumbs for they lunch. Good idea, yes, my Isabella?"

"A very good idea," I told him.
"Thank you, Mr. Cataloni."
And I did *not* look at his ears.

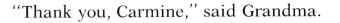

"Thank you, Carmine," said Grandma.

"*Niente*, Mrs. Da Costa. How you say? What she goes around, she comes back around again."

After lunch we sat in the sun a little, to warm up my
Grandma Rose's bones. We decided then and there that
even though Mr. Cataloni has hair coming out of his ears,
he is such a nice man I should give him one of my pictures.

"Where will we go next, Grandma?" I asked.

"Next, I think, Nadine," said Grandma. "Beautiful
paintings she does. But no cooking. She forgets to cook,
can you believe? So she gets soup. Once a week.
One day she says to me, 'Mrs. D., how can I thank you?
Your soup keeps me alive.' I tell her when she
gets famous she can paint my picture."

Grandma Rose was still laughing about that
when we got to Nadine's place and climbed up
all four floors. The door was open.

Nadine's place looked as if a bomb
had exploded in a paint store. And
there in the middle was Nadine,
in an overcoat.

"Nadine, I've got some soup for you," said my Grandma Rose, puffing.

"Mrs. D., you're an angel. I love you. Come in. Come in," shouted
Nadine. "Who is that small person behind you? Is that Isabel the Artist?
Come over where I can see you, small person," she hollered.

Nadine has wild and curly hair, and it's *purple*. Plus she has blue eyelids. She might have purple ears, too, but I couldn't see them, because she had on earmuffs. It was so cold I could see my breath in the room. Then I figured out that the earmuffs were why she was hollering.

"Are you Isabel the Artist, with all the pictures on her walls?" Nadine asked.

I nodded.

"Good," said Nadine. Then she rustled around in a corner. "I've been saving something for you. There. Open it."

I couldn't believe my eyes. Nadine was giving me her old paint box. With all the paints and brushes still in it.

"Nadine, are you sure?"
my Grandma Rose wanted to know.

"Of course, Mrs. D.," said Nadine. "Isabel, your grandma is a rare woman. In her bag, she brings me the elixir of life. In her heart, she brings me love. *Ciao*, Mrs. D., and thanks."

"Oh, pooh," my Grandma Rose said.

"Thank you, Nadine," I said.

Right then and there, I decided that even though Nadine had purple hair and hollered, she was one of the nicest people I knew. And I told my Grandma Rose I was going to make a special picture, just for Nadine. With lots of colors.

"What a wonderful idea, my pumpkin," said my Grandma Rose.

"Where to next?" I asked when we were back on the street.

"Just down the block a little. You know Mr. Klopnik's store?" asked Grandma.

Mr. Klopnik's store has to be my favorite store in the whole
wide world. There is so much stuff in his tiny store that
Mr. Klopnik stands outside, almost every day. I don't think
there's enough room for him inside.

"The reason that Mr. Klopnik
needs my soup is Mrs. Klopnik,"
Grandma Rose told me. "She's
terribly sick. So sick she is that she
never steps foot out of her bed.
All the day long while Mr. Klopnik
works in the store, she lies in her
bed by the window."

Sure enough, when we got to the store,
there was Mrs. Klopnik at the window,
waving to Grandma.

And there was Mr. Klopnik out in front, just as if he knew
we were coming, smiling his big smile that stretched his cheeks
almost back to his ears. Mr. Klopnik doesn't have any teeth.
"Another good reason for him to have soup," my Grandma Rose
said. "No chewing involved."

"Good afternoon, dear ladies," he boomed at us.
"Oh, Mrs. Da Costa. Don't tell me. You brought
soup? You have answered my prayers.
My Ruthie will want to see you.
Please, please, go in."

"I'll only be a moment, Isabel, my lamb chop," said
Grandma Rose. "You look around Mr. Klopnik's store,
and see if there's anything we can buy for your poor
sick mama, while I go say hello to dear Mrs. Klopnik."

Grandma went to their room, and the minute she was out of sight, Mr. Klopnik came over and whispered to me, "Isabel, you put your pennies away right this minute. I have saved something for you to give to your dear Grandma Rose.
It is a present from you
and the Klopniks."

From behind his desk, he pulled out *the most beautiful bag* I'd ever seen.

"Now, Isabel," he said. "Don't you think your Grandma Rose could use this new bag? For her soups?" And Mr. Klopnik gave me his smile. It was the bag of my dreams! I knew Grandma Rose would love it. Red and purple; her favorite colors.

"Thank you, Mr. Klopnik," I told him. "It is perfect."

"Fine," said Mr. Klopnik. "Fine, my little Isabella. We roll this up and wrap it in a hurry, so that your grandmama, she doesn't see. That way it's a surprise, right?

Now, if only I could surprise my dear Ruthie with something. She is so lonely all day, nothing to look at."

Mr. Klopnik's face had started to look all sad, and sort of squinched up.

"Do you think," I said, "do you think that Mrs. Klopnik would like one of my pictures for her wall? Where she could look at it from her bed?"

Mr. Klopnik's face got all shiny
and bright with smiles.

"Oh, my Isabel," he said,
"from heaven you must be.
Such a *wonderful girl you are* with your ideas.
How can you do it?"

Right then and there, I decided
that even though he had no teeth,
Mr. Klopnik was one of the nicest
people I knew. And maybe from
looking at his happy smile get bigger
and bigger, my idea started
to get bigger and bigger.

"I know," I told him. "I, Isabel the Artist, will make Mrs. Klopnik
a new picture for her wall, every week."

I don't know who was more surprised,
Mr. Klopnik or me. We started
making such a racket of happiness
that Grandma Rose came out of
Mrs. Klopnik's room.

"Ssshhh. Mr. Klopnik. Isabel. Such a noise. Yes, a happy noise, but still, a noise. Mrs. Klopnik is resting now. Can you two nudniks settle down? Such a business. What's happening?" asked Grandma Rose.

Mr. Klopnik was smiling and wiping his eyes and trying to breathe, all at the same time, so I told Grandma Rose about our deal, and why we were so happy.

"Isabel, my gumdrop, you keep this up, you'll be needing a bag of your own one of these days. Right, Mr. Klopnik?" she said.

Mr. Klopnik gave me his special smile.

"Right, Mrs. Da Costa," he said.

I just smiled, thinking about my grandma's new bag.

"Now," said Mr. Klopnik, "I want you two lovely ladies should pick out surprises for Isabel's mama, who shouldn't be sick another minute. Each of you pick something to cheer her up, so she should be right away better."

"From your mouth to
God's ear, Mr. Klopnik,"
said my Grandma Rose.

In five minutes, Grandma
and I found just what
we wanted for my mama,
a beautiful blue boa
and a straw hat.

Mr. Klopnik wrapped up our surprises.

"Put your money away, dear Mrs. Da Costa," he said. "Your soup brings light to my Ruthie's eyes, and now we'll have Isabel's pictures, too. We are overcome by your kindnesses."

"It is you who are kind,
Mr. Klopnik, and thank you,"
said Grandma. "And what is that
other package you are giving me?"

My Grandma Rose misses nothing!

"Never mind," I told her.
"That's my private business,
Grandma. Me and Mr. Klopnik."
And I put it right in the
bag with the other two.

"Hah," said my Grandma Rose. "Surprises all over the place.
All right, Isabella, my little orange blossom, we must be
on our way. One more stop. Thank you, Mr. Klopnik,
and enjoy your soup."

"But, Grandma Rose," I said, "how can we have only one more stop?
Your old green bag weighs nearly a *ton*!"

"So, unbelieving child," she said, "do you still not get it?

If you have treasures, you must give away. So your house does not get too full of treasures to let in love. So you give away, and what do you know, you have more. I can't explain. It's what goes around . . ."

"I know," I said, "comes around."

"Yes, my pumpkin," said Grandma Rose. "Come, let's go see Harry."

I'd never *seen* Harry, but Grandma Rose was always talking about him. They dance together.

"See, there, my little twinkle-toes,"
said Grandma Rose. "The window on
the corner. Can you read the sign?"

"Yes," I answered. "It says HARRY, DANCE INSTRUCTOR TO THE STARS."

"That's it," said my grandma. "Our last stop. Just on the
next block. All alone, Harry is, and he works so hard
teaching the stars to dance, he can't be bothered to eat.
Hot dogs he lives on, can you believe? So he gets soup.
Every week. And for that, he lets your old Grandma Rose
dance on his waxed floor."

We knocked on the door, and Harry opened it.

"Rose, my queen," he said. "You are just in time. Can you stay?
I will dust off the old records. Ho! Who is this princess
you have with you? Is this Isabel, of whom I have heard nothing but
wondrous things? Isabel, the *Artiste Extraordinaire*?"

"The very one, Harry, this is she," said Grandma Rose.

Then Harry took Grandma Rose and me by the hand and led us
into his back room. "Change," he told us. "Rose, you show
Isabel where everything is. Pick out something ravishing to
wear, and find some shoes. Today, Harry is among the luckiest.
Two partners. Oh mymymymy."

I have never seen anything like Harry's back room. There were costumes and outfits, shoes, fans, hats, even batons. I thought I'd gone to heaven. Grandma and I found our best outfits.

"Ooh, Grandma Rose. You are beautiful."

"Hurry, my pumpkin," said Grandma.
"Harry will be waiting. Listen.
Hear the music?"

"Let's dance to some old tunes, my long-legged beauties,"
said Harry. "What'll it be first?"

"Oh, Harry," said Grandma Rose. "Play 'Let Me Call You Sweetheart.'"

Then we danced and danced.

"Like Broadway we are," said Grandma Rose. "Just like Broadway."

At last Grandma Rose collapsed in a chair.
"My stars, Harry," she said. "Ginger Rogers I'm not.
It's old I am today."

Harry bowed low, and tipped his hat. "Old is in your head, Rose,
not your heart," he said. "And definitely not in your feet."

I knew right away why Harry wore his hat all the time. His head
was as bald and shiny as the glass egg Grandma used for mending.

"So, Rose, how's the soup business these days?" asked Harry.

"Oh, Harry, you made me forget all about the soup," said my
Grandma Rose. "I brought you some, of course. In the bag."

Then Harry threw his arms around my Grandma Rose, picked her up, and whirled her around the floor.

"Rose, Rose," he said. "The fairest flower that grows. Rose, you must marry me. Tomorrow. Today. And if you won't marry me, then at least you must promise to come dance with me once a week without fail. And bring Isabel, too. And if you could see your way clear to bring along some soup, then I would be the happiest of men."

I could hardly believe my ears. Harry wanted me to come and practice dancing with him and Grandma Rose.

"For you, Isabel," Harry said. "A pair of Magical Dancing Shoes. Practice, Isabel the Artist. Harry, Instructor to the Stars, means business."

I was so happy I hugged Harry myself. Right then and there, I decided that Harry needed my services as *Artiste Extraordinaire*. The walls in his studio were *bare*. They needed some of my *biggest* pictures.

After we changed, we all hugged good-bye.

I told Grandma Rose that even though
Harry had no hair, I thought he was
one of the nicest people I knew, and
from now on, he was going to have
some of my pictures on his wall.

Grandma Rose said, "So, my Isabella. A bag lady
you'll be, like your grandma."

Harry was still waving to us
from his window when we turned
the corner toward home.

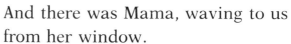

And there was Mama, waving to us
from her window.

"Oh, my sweetest one. You look
so much better. Your eyes, they
have sparkle back. What was it
made you get better so fast?"
said Grandma Rose, all at once.

"Must have been your soup, Mama.
Magic, like always. My word,
what have you two been up to?
Look at your bag. Bigger than ever.
I thought you were giving soup *away*?
What is in there?"

One by one, Grandma and I unpacked the packages from the bag. First came the orange and apple from Mr. Cataloni. Then, from Mr. Klopnik, the blue boa and straw hat. Mama put them right on, nightgown and all.

Then I showed her my paint box from Nadine. "That's nothing, Mama," I told her. "Look at my new dancing shoes. I have to practice because Harry, Instructor to the Stars, wants *me* to dance with him, every week."

Mama looked a little worried.

"Mr. Cataloni gave us lunch, Mama. And Mr. Klopnik and I have a big surprise for you, Grandma Rose." And I showed her the new purple and red bag, with stars. Grandma Rose laughed until she had tears in her eyes.

Mama looked *very* worried.

"What is it, my sweet one?" cried my Grandma Rose,
when she saw Mama's face.

"Mama. So much you and Isabel spent. The shoes. The boa.
The hat. Even the paint box. More than you have, I know it."

Grandma Rose put her arms around my mama. I crawled in close, too.

"Don't you know it was the miracle again," said Grandma Rose.
"We empty the bag, and somehow the bag fills up again. And as
full as the bag gets, fuller than that gets my heart."

"Starting tomorrow, I begin making
pictures for all my new friends,"
I told them. "I, Isabel the Artist,
will need the old green bag, please."

Grandma Rose gave me her proudest smile,
and Mama gave me a big hug.

"And now, I have some dancing practice to do,"
I told them. "What's for dinner?"

"Soup," said my Grandma Rose. "What else?"